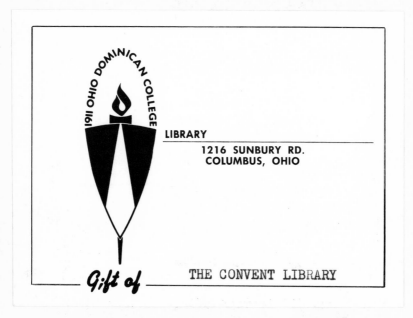

Jimmy and Joe
Get a Hens' Surprise

Jimmy and Joe Get a Hens' Surprise

by Sally Glendinning

paintings by Paul Frame

GARRARD PUBLISHING COMPANY
CHAMPAIGN, ILLINOIS

72063

Jimmy and Joe
Get a Hens' Surprise

Jimmy and Joe were playing ball.
It would soon be time
to go to school.
Jimmy's father called to them.
"Boys, I have a surprise
for each of you," he said.

The boys came running.
Jimmy's father held a box
in each hand.
Inside each box
was a little gray hen.
"One is for you, Joe,"
he said.
"And one is for Jimmy."
"What a surprise, Dad!"
shouted Jimmy.
"Thank you," cried Joe.
"These are Araucana hens,"
Jimmy's father said.
"They will give you a surprise."

"What are Araucana hens?"
asked Joe.
"Araucana hens do something
no other hens can do,"
Jimmy's father said.
The boys opened the boxes.
Out flew the hens.

The hens flew to the top
of a little tree.
"Our hens flew away!"
cried Joe.
"We must catch them!"
cried Jimmy.
"Help us, Dad."

"The hens like corn,"
Jimmy's father said.
He took a bag of corn
from his pocket.
He put some corn
into each of the boxes.
Then he put in some sand.

The hens flew down
and hopped into the boxes.
"They are eating the sand!"
cried the boys.
"Hens have no teeth,"
Jimmy's father said.
"They use sand for teeth!"

"Use sand for teeth!"
laughed Jimmy.
"That's a surprise!"
"That's not the BIG surprise,"
Jimmy's father said.
"The hens will give you
a BIG surprise."
"I must go to work now,"
Jimmy's father said.
He told the boys good-bye,
and walked down the street.
"Let's take the hens
with us to school,"
said Joe.

The hens hopped on the grass.
They looked for bugs to eat.
A big dog ran to the hens.
He barked at them.
"Go away, you bad dog!"
cried Joe.
"You will hurt the hens!"
cried Jimmy.

The hens flew at the dog
and pecked him on the head.
The dog ran away.
Then the hens hopped back
into their boxes.
It was time to go to school.

The boys walked to the street
where the school bus stopped.
The bus driver looked
at the hens in the boxes.
"No pets on the school bus!"
the driver said.

"Please!" cried Joe.

"These are surprise hens,"
said Jimmy.

The bus driver laughed.

"All right," she said.

"Keep the hens in the boxes."

The boys climbed onto the bus.

All the children in the bus
wanted to see the hens.
"Sit down! Sit down!"
cried the bus driver.
So the children sat down.
The bus went to the school.
The children climbed down
from the school bus.
"May we play with the hens?"
they asked Jimmy and Joe.
Then the school bell rang.
There was no time to play.
The boys took the gray hens
to their classroom.

"Good morning, boys,"
said the teacher.
"These are surprise hens,"
said Jimmy.
"They are Araucana hens,"
Joe said.
"ARAUCANA HENS?"

asked the teacher.
"They will give you
a real surprise!"
The children tried to guess
what the surprise would be.
"Just wait and see!"
said the teacher.

The children read books
and sang songs.
"Cluck, cluck," sang the hens.
"Open the boxes, boys,"
said the teacher.
The boys opened the boxes,
and out flew the hens.

The hens flew in the air,
flapping their wings.
They flew around the room.
One hen flew to Joe's head
and sat there to rest.
The other flew to Jimmy
and sat on his head.

"It's time for show and tell,"
said the teacher.
She asked Jimmy and Joe
to tell about the hens.
The boys held up the hens
so the children could see them.
"Dad gave us the hens,"
said Jimmy.
"They flew to the top
of a tree," said Joe.
"They like to eat corn,"
said Jimmy.
"They pecked a big dog,"
Joe said.

"The gray hens need nests,"
said one of the children.
"Let's make nests for them,"
the teacher said.
"We will make nests of paper."
She gave yellow paper to the boys
and red paper to the girls.

The children tore the paper
into very small bits.
They made a red paper nest
and a yellow paper nest.
One hen sat in the red nest.
One sat in the yellow nest.
They went to sleep.

"Now it's time to play,"
said the teacher.
The children went out
to the playground.
The boys played ball.
The girls jumped rope.
What fun they had!

They stood in line
to go down the slide.
They tried the see-saw.
All of the children
had a good time.
Then they went back
to the classroom.

There sat the hens on the nests.
"CLUCK, CLUCK," said the hens.
"CLUCK, CLUCK, CLUCK!"
"Maybe they want some water,"
said Jimmy.
He got some water
in a little cup.
"CLUCK, CLUCK!" said the hens.
"Maybe they want some corn,"
Joe said to the teacher.
He got some corn
from his pocket.
But the little gray hens
didn't eat any corn.

The teacher laughed.

"Soon the gray hens will give you
the BIG surprise," she said.

The teacher opened a book.

She read about hens
to the children.

She read about Araucana hens.

She said that Araucana hens
were first kept by the Indians.
But she didn't tell
what the surprise would be.
She called Jimmy and Joe.
"Look in the nests, boys,"
the teacher said.

Joe went to the yellow nest.
Jimmy went to the red nest.
They picked up the hens.
They looked into the nests.
"Hens' surprise!" they cried.
"Here is the hens' surprise!"

"What is the surprise?"
called the children.
"Let us see! Let us see!"
"Sit down, children,"
said the teacher.
"Let Jimmy and Joe tell us
about the surprise."

"My surprise is an egg,"
said Jimmy.
"I have an egg, too," said Joe.
"Ha, ha," laughed the children.
"That's no surprise.
All hens lay eggs."
"But this egg is GREEN!"
cried Joe.
"This egg is BLUE!"
shouted Jimmy.
They held up the eggs
for the children to see.
Joe's egg was grass green.
Jimmy's egg was sky blue.

"Other hens lay white eggs
or brown eggs,"
the teacher said.
"Araucana eggs are green
or even blue.
Sometimes there may be
an egg with a pink shell."

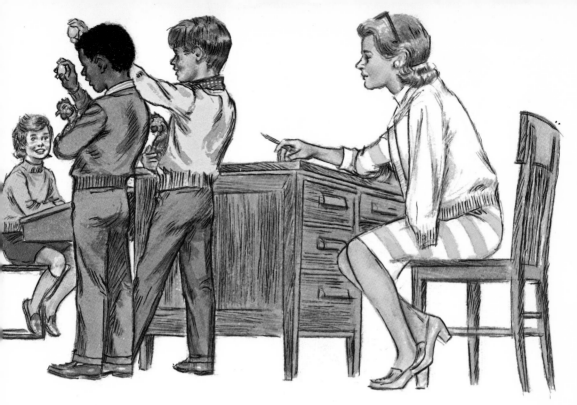

A little boy looked
at Joe's green egg.
"Is the inside green?"
he asked the teacher.
"No," said the teacher.
"Only the shell is green.
The inside is yellow and white."

Jimmy and Joe put the hens
into their boxes.
It was time to go home.
"Thank you, Jimmy and Joe!"
cried the children.
"Thank you for showing us
the hens' surprise."

Date Due

MAR 4 '74				
MR 11 '74				
MY 15 '74				
DC 9 '74				
MAR 0 1 '81				
JUL 6 '84				